Christmas Pie

A Sweet Slice of Christmas

by

Agnes Geraldine Davis

North America & international
toll-free: 1 888 232 4444 (USA & Canada)
phone: 250 383 6864 ♦ fax: 812 355 4082

ACKNOWLEDGMENTS

Illustrations are by Chanit Roston

Cover design is by Agnes Geraldine Davis

Chestnuts roasting on an open fire and the beauty of the evergreen tree have long established their iconic place in yuletide lyrics. While they help to enkindle the materialistic aspects of the holiday, one cannot help but wonder what has happened to the divine proclamation, '*Glory to God in the Highest, Peace on Earth, Goodwill to Men*'? Given rise to the ever increasing global turmoil, it seems that these latter ingredients have drastically diminished, thus altering the true meaning of Christmas within ourselves. Weaving spirituality, humor, intelligence, insight - - and most of all *love* into the fabric of human experience, the author has written an anthology of short stories that embrace the true essence of Christmas. No matter what your age, if you love Christmas you will love *Christmas Pie.*

Christmas Lore - - depicts a more simplistic, old fashioned style of holiday celebration. *On Our Way to Christmas* follows a brother and sister's journey in search of Christmas. *St. Nicholas Day* captures our heart with the kindness and thoughtfulness of a little girl. *A Christmas Wish* portrays the power of prayer. *Little Lost Fawn* spotlights family togetherness while caring for a wounded animal. *The Legend of the Tree* examines suffering and redemption. *Christmas in the Country* exposes the humorous side of one feisty mare. *The Skater's Ball* is a beautiful example that a good deed is never forgotten.

To My Friend,
Marie.
Thank you for encouraging my writing endeavors -
You are always in my thoughts.
And
To All the World
A Christmas Gift List
From Oren Arnold:

"To your enemy - forgiveness
To an opponent - tolerance
To a friend - your heart
To a customer - service
To all - charity
To every child - a good example
To yourself - respect"

Merry Christmas to all - and to all, love and a good right!

Christmas Lore

Red and green candles burning bright,
Flickering flames dance with delight!
Gifts directly from Kris Kringle's door,
Who could want for anything more?
Crackling fireplaces, carolers singing
"O Holy Night" "The Christmas Song"!
Chestnuts roasting on an open fire, warm apple cider,
Eggnog spiced with fruited brandy.
Shimmering icicles, two wheeled bicycles,
Wreaths of holly - - and mistletoe, too
Children making merry – children making folly
As in all the years before.

Mother and I at the piano,
Father, brother and sister, too,
Caroling in our Christmas debut.
Homemade biscuits, apple strudel,
Rhubarb pie — turkey in the oven,
"Silent Night" " O Tannenbaum"
Beautifully sung by Nat King Cole
Now a memory of past sung lore.
Who could want for anything more?

Ah, yes - my dearest family, my dearest friends,
There is but one thing more.
Tis a Christmas wish - a Christmas prayer
From my heart to you and yours,
For a most blessed, a most beautiful,
A most joyous Christmas Season.
In this, my festive Christmas Lore

Chapter 2

On Our Way to Christmas

The virgin snow spread before us like one magnificent jewel, faceted by the silvery smile drawn upon the evening sky. My brother and I, with childlike wonder, trod upon the glistening snow, trembling not from winter's cold, but from wondrous tales of old. We were on our way to Christmas! In the distance angelic voices were heard caroling, "All is calm, all is bright." Hand in hand our journey took flight on this wintry solstice night.

Out of the bushes there suddenly appeared a small, speckled reindeer. "Could Christmas be here"? I asked. "I don't think so", my brother said. "If Christmas were here, Santa's Elves would be in his workshop making toys for all the world's little girls and boys. There is nothing here but bushes and snow. We have a long, long way to go".

Earth's heavenly blanket stretched all around our beckoning landscape. Our eyes searched and searched, but Christmas could not be found. Again, out of the watchful eye of the moonlit sky, an angel appeared and proclaimed: "Hark, I bring you tidings of great joy, glory to God in the highest, peace on earth, goodwill toward men." I've heard that message again and again", my brother exclaimed! "So have I", was my reply. "Christmas must be close. Do the angels mean goodwill toward men regardless of race, color or creed"? Brother asked. "Yes, that is the meaning of Christmas. We have found Christmas!" was my ecstatic cry! "Christmas is here, Christmas is everywhere! Christmas can be celebrated every day of the year. It is the spirit of peace, love, joy and brotherhood that man holds in his heart"!

The snow suddenly began to melt and the pristine landscape quickly disappeared.
The small, speckled reindeer faded from sight, as I felt a soft, gentle kiss upon my cheek. It had awakened me from my searching sleep. Mother stood smiling over me as she uncovered my bed. Softly she said, "Wake up, my little angel, it's Christmas"!

Chapter 3
A Christmas Wish

The snow capped mountains glistened in the distance like large, unpolished diamonds. Their valley below lay resplendent with miles of pine, providing an endless terrain of timber. After Thanksgiving, father promised a family sojourn into this unspoiled countryside to select our holiday tree.

On the morning of our departure, a light blustery snow began to fall. I watched the snowflakes swirl in the wind, like tiny white butterflies, while our horse drawn sleigh plowed through the powdered countryside. The mountains, barely visible through their shimmering veil, imparted an aura of mystery. Mother and I were cuddling under our blanket when she took a letter from her pocket addressed to Santa. She smiled and said, "Theresa, I have a wonderful surprise for you."

The trees stood tall and proud in the shadow of the mountains, like soldiers defying the wilderness. Before *Old Jingles* came to a halt, I jumped onto the snow and ran over to a tall, perfectly shaped evergreen. "Over here father," I shouted, "Look at this one, isn't it beautiful?" My voice echoed in the wind as I pointed to a silver needled pine. "Please, father, can we have this one"? After father had felled the tree, he planted another to replace it. "Always give thanks and give back whenever you can," he had taught me, "for that fulfills the universal law of giving and receiving."

The statuesque pine was placed next to the parlor mantel filling the room with its perfumed breath. When my friends arrived for the tree trimming party several days later, a light hearted rivalry began. "Please can I put the star on top?" asked Christopher. "No, let me, let me!" shouted Katherine. To be fair, mother explained, all names would be put into an elf's hat, and the name drawn would be the winner.

Laughter, music and a delicious aroma filled the air! Everyone clapped when Katherine's name was pulled from the hat. Giggling, she sat on father's shoulders and proudly placed the star on top. When the tree was trimmed and the lights turned on, hushed sighs filled the room. The tree dazzled in its display of brilliant white lights and twinkling star. The twelve days of Christmas had begun!

When the last spoonfuls of Christmas pudding were eaten, Santa arrived with a sack full of toys. My friends hurriedly opened their gifts and began to play - everyone except Sari. She sat quietly by the tree watching - - her Santa doll lay on the floor, beside her.

The day came to an end all too quickly as a yellow bus pulled up and tooted its horn. It had been a wonderful day. Mother hugged each one as my friends began to scramble onto the bus. When Sari got on, she sat in the front seat next to Katherine. Mother commented that she wasn't carrying her doll. When the bus driver went to the back of the bus to take count, Sari suddenly jumped off and stood in the snow, waving to us. Everyone laughed and applauded as the bus driver jumped off the bus, scooped her up in his arms and trotted playfully around in the snow - then putting Sari on his shoulders before he placed her back into her seat.

During our journey into the country, mother had read aloud Sari's letter to Santa.

Dear Santa,
My name is Sari. I don't want any toys for Christmas. I just want to be adopted. Theresa got adopted and doesn't live at the orphanage anymore. She was my best friend. I miss her very much. We always played together. She taught me how to sing Rudolph the Red Nosed Reindeer, and she read me stories every night at bedtime. I wish her mommy and daddy would adopt me, too, so she would be my sister.
Love, Sari

Mother and I smiled as Sari was put onto the bus again. Our hearts were full of joy, for we knew this would be her last bus ride back to the orphanage. Her Santa doll was placed under the tree, waiting to greet her on Christmas morning!

Chapter 4
Little Lost Fawn

The north wind blew through the trees splashing clumps of snow against the window panes. The shutters shook and rattled in their winded frenzy, as Sari slipped out of bed and tiptoed across the room. I peeked out from under the blankets as she put on her snowsuit and boots. What was my little sister up to now, before breakfast? When she left the room, I sprang to the window and watched as she unlatched the garden gate and disappeared into the crisp morning air. I quickly dressed and followed her snow tracks to the sleigh shed. As I drew closer, I heard "You'll go down in historrreeeee" ring through the air in its familiar flat pitch. When I entered the shed, Sari was sitting in the back of the sleigh singing to her lap.

"What are you doing, Sari, who are you singing to?" "Sssh, Theresa, you'll scare him," she whispered, her forefinger poised to her lips. "I'm singing to Rudolph, Santa's reindeer. I found him here, yesterday. Look, he has a cut on his leg. I'm trying to make him better." I laughed when I saw one leg wrapped in Sari's red scarf, tied in a big bow. "Will you help me make him better?" she asked. The fawn looked up at me with his large, brown liquid eyes. "Yes, I'll help you, but why do you think he belongs to Santa?" "You're silly, Theresa, can't you see his nose is red and it glows," she replied. I looked closely at his nose, but it was as black as a lump of Christmas coal! "When he's all better, we'll write to Santa and let him know he's here. Santa must be very worried." "Yes, very worried," I mumbled to myself. "Sari, we must tell mother and father about Rudolph, so they can help us." "Yes, I suppose so," she replied.

Each morning everyone gathered in the shed to care for Sari's wounded mascot. I fed him bottles. Mother cleaned and dressed his wound. Father taught us which berries and foliage to gather from the woods. Sari continued to serenade him with his song. He seemed to love Sari's singing, for each time she'd finish, he would look up at her and kiss the tip of her nose. Sari would giggle and begin singing all over again! Soon Rudolph was able to romp and play outdoors. He frolicked in the snow, chased blowing leaves and nibbled happily on the bushes. It seemed Rudolph was now ready to go back to the North Pole. One night mother announced, "Girls, Christmas is only two weeks away.
We must write to Santa tonight so that he will get our letter before Christmas.
He needs Rudolph to help guide his sleigh so he can deliver presents to all the good little boys and girls around the world." "Yes, mother," we nodded.

Now that he was well, Rudolph appeared outside our bedroom window every morning, waiting for us to get up. However, he didn't seem to be as happy as he once was. After he ate his berries, he trotted back to the sleigh shed and curled up in his blanket. He no longer frolicked in the snow, or chased the blowing leaves. When Sari sang to him, he lowered his head in her lap and closed his eyes.

When Christmas Eve morning arrived, Rudolph wasn't waiting outside our window. Heartbroken, Sari and I ran to the sleigh shed to look for him. He wasn't there. We looked everywhere, but Rudolph was nowhere to be found! Mother tried to console us. She said that we had done a wonderful deed by caring for him, but now that he was well, he had probably gone back to the North Pole. Mother promised that Santa would reward us for our goodness, but Sari and I wouldn't listen and kept looking for him.

When Sari awakened early Christmas morning, she found a letter from Santa under her pillow. It read:

Dear Sari and Theresa,

What good little girls you are! Thank you for taking care of Rudolph, Jr., (my elves call him "Dolphie"). I know you've heard of his famous father, Rudolph, Sr., who leads my sleigh on Christmas Eve. I'm not certain how it happened, but right after Thanksgiving, as I was fitting each deer for a new harness, Dolphie strayed from my workshop. He wanted to be fitted, too, in order to pull the sleigh next to his father on Christmas Eve. I told him that he was still too little. He trotted away looking very sad, and - POOF - in the blink of an Elf's eye, he disappeared. My elves quickly constructed a super hi-tech telescope, with a lunar-bright, world-wide lens, so I could look for him. Before I could say, "fiddle-dee-dee-where-in-the-world-is my little Dolphie," I sighted him in your sleigh shed. I knew he was in good hands.
But when he came back to the North Pole, he was a changed little deer. He no longer wanted to draw my sleigh with his father. When I harnessed up the team, he watched from afar as my elves loaded the sleigh.
Ho, ho, ho, when I landed on your roof-top Christmas Eve - - I got a very big surprise!
Santa Claus

After Sari opened her gifts on Christmas morning, she wheeled her doll carriage into the bedroom. Suddenly I heard "*You'll go down in historrreeeee*" ring through the air. I ran into the bedroom and saw Sari singing through the opened window. There stood Rudolph outside the garden gate, nibbling happily on the bushes. His nose was glowing and, indeed, it was red.

Chapter 5
Christmas in the Country

Winter in the country has a magical quality that is unequaled by her sister seasons. Soon after harvest, the land is transformed and slumbers peacefully under a sea of snow, inviting a playful mood that even our equine friends can't resist. Watching horses thunder through the snow, free and wild, exhilarated by the feel of cold powder beneath their hooves is a spectacular winter sight.

At the stroke of sunset, the countryside glows with lights that flicker like fireflies, lighting the way for Santa and his eight tiny reindeer! Christmas in the country is the sparkling jewel in winter's wand in our little hamlet, for it is celebrated with pageantry and merriment, filling hearts with joy and good-will . . . and lights that mischievous twinkle in Santa's eye!

Morning light spilled softly across the small stream, announcing a new day. 'All is calm - all is white', I mused, as I peered out at the glistening snow. I could almost hear the God of Darkness sigh a lament, as nocturnal shadows surrendered to the rising sun. Arabesque and Gingersnap, my favorite fillies, were already in rendezvous with the new day. An inseparable pair of equine rebels, they had wandered from the herd to drink at their favorite refreshment stand. Father calls their liquid oasis, 'The farm's little miracle,' for it refuses to freeze.

Today marks the twelfth day before Christmas. Our town traditionally opens the holiday season on this day with a Christmas pageant. The festivities are scheduled to commence at noon, with a procession of horse drawn sleighs, decorated in holiday regalia. This year, I entered Arabesque and Gingersnap into the competition. A prize would be awarded for the most original sleigh ornamentation and equine performance. My two fillies would draw our beautifully restored French antique sleigh, now fit for Louis XIV. Decorated from bob to blade with colored lights, jingle bells and garlands, the sleigh stood in waiting for its four legged mascots.

The morning sun was now firmly fixed in the sky, and the family would soon gather in the stables to help groom the fillies. Their manes would be braided with red and green ribbons. Each would sport a decorated top hat. Pompoms, jingle bells and garlands of holly would be affixed to their harnesses.

Snap, (so called for she would snap at anything in sight when her mischievous mood arose), was unusually playful this morning. She sensed something was different, for her rebellious spirit broke into full mode. She tried to swipe everything in sight and kept nudging toward Ara, as though imploring her aid to escape from this strange grooming session. After much cajoling and many carrots later, the fillies were decorated from muzzle to hoof for their parade debut.

The notes of the bugle resounded throughout the park, officially opening the Christmas festivities. One by one, the sleighs moved onto their given positions. I was bursting with pride as Ara and Snap began their grand trot toward the judge's podium. Suddenly the crowd began to stir as they pointed toward our sleigh! Stretching my stance, I saw Snap trying to catch the pompom affixed to her harness. Her head kept bobbing and twisting toward her left side, as she kept snapping at the air with her teeth. She was putting on quite an exhibition as she puckered and contorted her muzzle with the deftness of an animated cartoon. The crowd and I were in an uproar!

"What is this silly thing hanging from my bit? I don't like it swinging against my muzzle - somehow I've got to get it off. Drats, if it would only stop moving, I could grab it. Oops - I missed again." Subsequently Snap's stride began to falter, interrupting her and Ara's rhythmic trot, adding to the chaotic comedy. "What's so funny? Why is everyone laughing at me? It must be this silly hat I'm wearing. I don't look good in hats . . . besides, it makes my ears stick out! That hunky stallion over there will never look at me, dressed like this! Whose idea was this, anyway? Get me out of here! I want to be free to gallop in the snow and drink in the quiet stream. Come on, Ara, when I give you the signal, let's make a run for it." Suddenly the sleigh took off and whizzed past the podium, stopping short at the entry gate. The crowd whistled, cheered and applauded as I sheepishly led the sleigh from the park.

Snap's shenanigans did not win us the coveted prize, but her performance made front page headlines in the town chronicle. My filly clown is still the talk of the town, especially at pageant time; always a reminder that Snap is definitely a horse of a different shade of ginger, right down to the very last laugh.

Chapter 6
The Legend of the Tree

aud's Bed and Breakfast stood like a beacon at the edge of Cautantowit Coos, punctuating the ebbing rhythm of the day. The moon of December hung in opalescent silence, promising nocturnal respite to the valley below. I closed my eyes and drifted back in space and time. It was as though I had slipped through a looking glass, into a Christmas past. Reminiscing, I yearned to stay there forever.

One Christmas long ago, White Loon, an Abenaki tribesman and grandmother's longtime caretaker, took my hand and led me to a particular pine tree at the edge of the Coos. It was the most beautiful tree I had ever seen! Dripping with brilliant blue color that spilled onto the snow, we stood silently in the deep cold, bedazzled by its beauty.

"This tree has a wonderful story," White Loon began. "Cautantowit, the God of all living things, has blessed this tree with a strong spirit.

Many moons ago, when I was a young forest ranger, a great wildfire raged for days throughout this area of the White Mountains. It destroyed most of the trees in its path. However, this tree survived. The spirit of Cautantowit protected it. The great god then ordered the wind to blow its pollinated seedlings onto the earth, so new pines would grow. When new shoots began to burst forth, my people rejoiced and honored Him by naming this road, Cautantowit Coos. The name means, "God's pine trees filling up the landscape."

Sometime after the fire, the forest was plagued by mountain beetles. The tree was attacked, but, again, it survived. Then the year I came to work for your grandmother, a severe drought destroyed much of the forest. The tree looked sad with so many brown and brittle needles. Slowly, it blossomed into full green life, once again. Pine needle scale followed. Through it all, this tree stood strong and steadfast.

One day I pondered, what is so special about this tree? The Abenaki believe that everything on earth has a consciousness, even trees. They also believe that pine trees have great healing powers. When I was young, I did not believe the teachings of my people. I was a rebel. Before you were born, I suffered a great heartache.

Strangely, I found myself drawn to this tree. Many nights, I would sit in the moonlight contemplating my life, searching for answers. The answers would suddenly come to me, in unexpected ways. Slowly I began to believe the teachings of my people. My heart began to heal. You will come to know, Dawn Princess, that everything in life has a purpose, even suffering. Suffering scours the heart. Suffering transforms the heart. This tree is very special to me. It is my symbol of courage and survival."

That night White Loon told me about the mystical and magical powers of the moon. Pointing toward the sky he said, "My people call the December moon Nuupapana. The name means night fire moon. It is the moon of suffering. It was here, by this tree, under the light of Nuupapana, many years ago, that your grandmother told me of your birth. It was at that moment that the Great Spirit entered and transformed my heart. It was the beginning of a new dawn for me. I honored that moment by naming you Dawn Princess."

White Loon also told me if ever I had a problem to come here and speak to the tree. He said, "Ask the tree questions and it will give you answers." Giggling, I had replied, "You're silly, White Loon, trees cannot talk". "No, you are right, trees cannot talk, but the answers will come to you in unexpected ways." His black eyes shone brightly with wisdom and mirth. His words flowed like silvery beads from the night fire moon, kindling love and joy in my tender heart. It was a wonderful story. It was a wonderful Christmas!

White Loon is now in the land of the Great Spirit. The moon of December hung high in the evening sky as I found my way to the tree. It stood before me, radiant in color and legendary glory, as though expecting me. The wind kissed my cheek as I stood silently in the cold.

"Ask the tree questions, and it will give you answers" echoed in my memory. "White Loon, where are you? Can you hear me"? Tears filled my eyes. "I miss you, White Loon. I miss your wonderful stories. You gave me the spiritual values that I live by today. I pray that Cautantowit will always protect this tree." Then I asked, "What heartache did White Loon suffer?" My eyes were fixed upon Nuupapana, as I listened for an answer. In the distance, I could hear the faint cry of a loon.

That night as I lay sleeping, White Loon appeared to me in a dream. Smiling, he said, "Dawn Princess, you are my beloved granddaughter." I awakened with a jolt and ran to the window, searching the night sky. Why would grandmother keep this a secret? Why did they never marry? His words played upon my mind like a haunting lullaby. The moon disappeared behind a cloud as I closed my eyes and drifted back in space and time, to an evening of long ago. A voice within me whispered, the answers are written in the legend of the tree.

Chapter 7

St. Nicholas Day

St. Nicholas Eve was here once again! I pranced all through the house, unable to contain the excitement that St. Nicholas Eve brings. I ran to the window to search the evening sky for the North Pole, hoping I would see St. Nicholas and his reindeer. I asked mother to show me how to find the North Pole. "Come Laura, come and sit next to me by the window and I'll help you find the North Pole. Now, look up into the sky and search for the brightest star. When you have found it, take your finger and draw a line straight up - - from the very top of the star - - to the very top of the sky, as far as you can see. There, beyond the clouds, beyond the sun and far beyond the moon, hidden in a special little place just below heaven, you will find the North Pole. Now, while you are searching, I'm going to go into the kitchen and get the cookies that you helped me bake for St. Nicholas," mother said as she left the room.

I was still searching for the brightest star when mother came back with the plate of cookies and a glass of milk. She placed them on a table next to the fireplace. "I think it may still be a little early" mother commented as she looked out at the sky. "All the stars haven't come out yet, but I think St. Nicholas is probably loading up his sleigh this very minute and getting ready for his long journey. Perhaps we should leave some carrots for his reindeer as well, don't you think"?

The snow glowed like burning embers as the sun slipped into the belly of the earth. The balsams, dressed in frosted white, shimmered in the deepening twilight. I was happy. St. Nicholas would soon be here! I hurried up the stairs and jumped into bed, anxious for morning to arrive.

Later mother came into my room and sat on the bed. She read my favorite Christmas story, "The Night Before Christmas" three times before I said my prayers. "Please St. Nicholas - please don't forget to bring the special gift that I asked you for. It's very important. Mommy said to be sure to tell you to have Rudolph guide your sleigh tonight, so the reindeer won't slip off our steep roof and cause a fright. Amen. Goodnight, St. Nicholas", I whispered. "Don't forget to eat the cookies that I helped mommy bake - and drink your milk.

Oh, I almost forgot, the carrots are for your reindeer." Mother then drew the covers over Teddy and me and tucked us in. "Sweet dreams" mother said as she kissed us goodnight. "Good night, mommy", I said, as I gave her a tight hug. When mother turned out the light, I closed my eyes and waited for sugar plums to dance in my head.

The curtains were bathed in soft sunlight as I awakened in the morning. Shadows of evergreen branches bounced on the wall casting curious patterns. I jumped out of bed and ran downstairs to look on the table. The cookies, carrots and milk were gone! I ran over to the tree and searched through the brightly colored packages. I reached for a gift that was tied with a large red bow. It read: *To Laura, a very good little girl.* I quickly untied the red satin ribbon and carefully opened the box. "Thank you, St. Nicholas, thank you", I shouted when I saw its contents. "I knew you wouldn't let me down".

I quickly got dressed and ran across the path to the house next door. Holding the gift tightly in my hands, I rang the door bell and waited impatiently for a freckled face boy to answer. Finally, Johnny came to the door in his wheelchair. "Hi, Johnny, Happy St. Nicholas Day, this is for you", I exclaimed, as I handed him the package.

I shall never forget the surprise and joy on Johnny's face that morning as I handed him the gift. The expression in his warm, brown eyes spoke silently to my soul with golden tongue.

Chapter 8
The Skater's Ball

The Skater's Ball – Millennium Year 2000

The bells of St. Mark's Cathedral began to chime as our carriage wound its way around the lake just outside of town. Its hallmark is the grand Winslow estate that stands serenely amid white birch trees that overlook the water.

Built in the late 19th century, it was fashioned after Versailles, complete with magnificent rose gardens, fountains and topiary that abound behind the stately structure. Victoria, the last surviving Winslow, married and moved abroad in 1935, bequeathing the estate to the town and its residents. The east wing of the estate was then transformed into an ice arena, aptly named The Victoria Palace, in tribute to Ms. Winslow's generous endowment and to commemorate her competition in the Olympics figure skating, having brought home the coveted gold. In spring and summer, the velvety verdant lawn is impeccably groomed; brightly colored umbrellas dot the expansive terrain shading white summer furniture that invites relaxation and casual dining.

Each year, on the eve of St. Nicholas, the festive Skater's Ball is held at The Victoria Palace to celebrate the Yuletide season. This year, as a tribute to the millennium, a candlelight procession will wind its way around the lake to the cathedral followed by fireworks over the lake. At midnight, the church bells will chime once again to announce the grand finale for this fairy tale event - candlelight mass - - followed by a visit from Old St. Nick!

Excitement filled the air as our carriage neared The Victoria Palace giving me butterflies. "You look beautiful", said my sister.
"Yes, Laura looks radiant in crimson," mother replied.

"I'm glad I was able to persuade her to wear my gown, for it had always brought me good luck, and it was the gown that I wore to my very first Skater's Ball. Beautiful memories are woven into that crimson fabric, Laura, and I wish you the same on this auspicious evening".

"Auspicious? Mother you never use that word unless you've had your hand in something and you're sure of the outcome. Do you know something that I don't – and you're not telling me? Maybe that's why I have butterflies. What if this gown doesn't prove to be lucky for me as it was for you"? I retorted.

Mother, in her most reassuring voice replied, "Nonsense Laura, call it a mother's intuition, but I just have a feeling this is not only going to be the most elaborate - but also the best Skater's Ball you have ever attended. So, relax my darling, for the evening is young and full of joyous festivities. As for having butterflies, remember, you always loved chasing them when you were a little girl. If one happened to fly onto your hand, you would squeal with delight and exclaim how beautiful the little creature was - - and then you would release it into the wind. Butterflies are still the same as they were when you were little – delicate, beautiful and harmless. Now, I want you to relax, close your eyes and take a deep breath. Then, as you exhale, release your butterflies into the wind. Be happy, Laura, you are going to have a wonderful time tonight, I just *feel* it"!

"Thank you, mother, I suppose I just needed to hear you say that".

The carriage drew to a halt and my little sister got out and joined her friends who were skating on the lake. As mother and I entered the palace, we marveled at the decorations. Thousands of tiny crimson lights twinkled from the ceiling and encircled the orchestra pit. I looked at mother and laughed. "Really mother, you have a strange sense of fashion! Now I see why you wanted me to wear your crimson gown - - so I would match the ceiling"!

Whatever apprehension I felt earlier melted in the lilt of mother's laughter and the warm glow of the room. I quickly laced my skates and glided across the ice. As I began skating, I noticed my sister at the window beckoning me to come outside. "What is it"? I asked, as she ran toward me.

"A photographer asked me to give this to you," and handed me a note. It read: *Hello, Lady in Red, I would be honored if you would save a waltz for me.*

 I was showing mother the mysterious message when a man across the room caught my glance and smiled. He was tall and very attractive wearing a dark suit with a red bow tie and dark, tousled hair. He appeared suave and continental but projected a pleasant and approachable demeanor. Though he held an air of familiarity, I was sure I had never seen him before. He skated toward me and greeted me in European fashion, kissing both sides of my cheek.

"Do I know you"? I queried.

"We knew each other a long time ago" was his reply.

Puzzled, I looked into his warm, brown eyes for a moment. A scene from my childhood flashed before me. I was standing on a porch holding a gift tied with a large red bow, waiting for a freckled face boy to answer the door. Could it be, I wondered?

 "Johnny"?? I asked, incredulously. "I don't believe it, is it *really you*"?

"Yes, it's me, minus the wheelchair and minus the freckles".

 "What a wonderful surprise! It's so nice to see you again. Whatever brings you to The Skater's Ball this evening"?

"Well, it's a bit of a story, which I'll explain later".

 "I remember we had just started taking skating lessons when you had the accident. I was 5, and you were" . . .

"I was 8," he interrupted.

"You look wonderful, Johnny - - you've grown so tall. It doesn't seem possible that its been 18 years since we've seen each other. I was really disappointed when your family moved away."

"Yes, I was disappointed, too, when my father told me he had accepted a job abroad, and that we would be moving right after the holidays. Given my hasty departure, the accident and my abashed shyness, I felt that I never had the opportunity to thank you properly and express my appreciation for your thoughtful gift. I vowed that as soon as I finished my studies, I would return."

"Johnny, there was no reason for you to have any regrets about your hasty departure. I admit that I was disappointed you were moving – and that we wouldn't be taking skating lessons together anymore – but my mother explained everything to me in a way that I understood and could accept."

"Well, I think you are lucky to have such a wonderful mother. Speaking about luck, moving abroad turned out to be very fortunate for me. They say everything happens for a reason.

I now agree with that wholeheartedly. The doctors here doubted that my foot would ever be strong enough for me to skate again - given the extent of the injury and nerve damage.

After several surgeries, my physicians abroad devised a new therapy treatment that would strengthen my foot. At first, I think even they were somewhat skeptical that I would skate again - but I proved them wrong. Ignoring the pain and frustration, I worked very hard for more than a year. Then one day I decided to try on the skates that you had given me, just to see if I could stand in them. With the help of my therapist, I slowly stood up. Even though I was weak and a bit shaky, at that moment, I knew I would someday skate again. I was overjoyed! Two years later, I resumed taking lessons and I haven't stayed away from the ice since. Well - - almost – - books played heavily in that scenario, as well. I didn't know it then, but the accident proved to be a blessing in disguise. It was the worst period in my life - - and it was the best. The accident completely changed who I was – and who I would become. The kindness and dedication from my doctors inspired me to study hard so I could become an orthopedic surgeon.

Laura, I want you to know that you, too, played a big part in my recovery. Honestly, if you hadn't given me the skates, I probably *wouldn't* have skated again. My world was suddenly turned upside down after the accident with my father announcing that we were moving abroad. It was like a bad dream and more than I could deal with. I had to start all over again and move to France where I didn't know anyone – or the language. My father assured me that I would learn French quickly, as he planned to hire a tutor – and, eventually I would attend the Sorbonne.

To make matters worse, dad said I couldn't bring my dog, Batman, with me. When I was in the wheelchair, Batman never left my side – he followed me wherever I went. My mother had to leave his food and water next to my chair, otherwise he wouldn't eat. Such devotion - so, you can well imagine how I felt when I couldn't bring him. Dad promised that my aunt Jane would take very good care of him. I loved that dog, and really missed him. I felt so alone without him. Because my father never had a pet was no reason to deprive me of having one. I was angry with him and I rebelled. Consequently, we didn't get along for quite a long time.

I can't explain it, Laura, but the skates seemed to hold some kind of mysterious and magical influence over me. They gave me the determination to get through the painful therapy period. At night, before going to bed, I would look at them and say to myself, *I am* going to skate again. Honestly, I think they heard me. The skates were always a reminder of back home and a life that I promised myself I would someday resume. And, now, 18 years later – that someday has arrived. Who said, "You can't go home again." It looks like I'm going to prove them wrong on that one too! So, with that said, Miss Lady in Red, you can't begin to imagine how much the skates helped me - - - - - -or *maybe* it was that large red bow!

Well, enough ancient history! Now I want to hear all about you and everything you have been up to throughout the past 18 years. Hmm, I think I'll need a few rain-checks since there isn't nearly enough time to do your story justice in one evening."

 "I can imagine how difficult it must have been for you, Johnny, especially during the painful therapy sessions - and without your dog. Sometimes parents lose sight of the strong bond that develops between a child and their pet, especially if they have never experienced the joy of having a pet themselves. I think that is probably what happened in your father's case. I understand how you must have felt, and, I know, through my own personal experience, that animals are a wonderful source of comfort. They never cease to amaze me. How they propel their sixth sense into one's orbit at just the perfect moment has always been a mystery to me. Someday I'll have to tell you about my cat, Cuddles, on one of your rain-checks.

I think you showed a great deal of strength and courage during such challenging and trying times - - at such a young age. You triumphed through it all, which tells a great deal about who you really are. I'm sure you will triumph in the medical field, as well.

As for the past 18 years of my life, I think those years will pale in comparison to yours. Having lived in the cosmopolitan setting of Paris and having been schooled at the Sorbonne is an extraordinary experience. I have always dreamed of visiting Paris, and then exploring the Alsace Lorraine region of France, where my maternal grandmother was born and raised – in a town called Nancy."

"Nancy!! That's amazing, Laura - - what a small world it's turning out to be! I know Nancy well, as I visited there a number of times. It's only an hour and 33 minutes by train from Paris.

I spent many Saturday afternoons in Nancy, rummaging through old book stores for hours on Le Grand Rue; then I would meander on to the magnificent Jardin de la Pépinière, where I relaxed and savored a glass of wine. And for the grand finale - a marvelous meal in one of my favorite bistros while waiting for La Place Stanislaus to light up in all its emblazoned architectural glory. Really a spectacular sight! After that, I'd make a mad dash to the train station and barely make the 9:52 back to Paris. That was my Saturday ritual whenever I visited Nancy. I hope you will get to visit the Alsace Lorraine region some day, Laura, especially Nancy - I think you will find it very charming and indescribably beautiful."

"Yes, I'm sure I will. When I was ten, my grandmother came to stay with us for a year. During her visit, she told me many stories about her childhood; how beautiful the countryside was and how she loved to run barefoot in the lush, green meadows and pick wild flowers. Every night before going to sleep, she would come into my bedroom and tell me another chapter about her girlhood and growing up in France. One night she told me the story about her pet hen that she named "Piaf," (after the French songstress, Edith Piaf).

Piaf followed her wherever she went. One day grandmother allowed Piaf to come into the house, since no one was home. The hen followed her into the bathroom. Suddenly, Piaf began to cluck hysterically. When grandmother looked to see what was wrong, low and behold, Piaf had laid an egg in the middle of the floor while grandmother was taking a bath! She said the hen was so proud of herself that she strutted all around the room with her wings spread out and wouldn't stop clucking! Then my grandmother got up and gave an impromptu impersonation of Piaf - strutting and clucking - flapping her arms wildly, as though she were in a theatrical performance. It was hilarious! I laughed myself to sleep that night and many nights thereafter, replaying grandmother's 'chicken dance'. It is, by far, the grandest memory I have of my grandmother. I adored her - she was warm, loving and caring – and at times, she could be a real hoot"!

"That's a great story! Your grandmother sounds like someone I would like to have known. You don't do too badly in the theatrical department yourself. For a moment, I thought you were going to do some strutting and clucking right here on the ice"! You relayed that story with such panache and comedic flair I daresay you have inherited your grandmother's 'hoot' gene".
"Very funny, Mr. Cavanaugh - but I do take that as a compliment."

"Yes, you should – I meant it as a compliment. Please continue, Laura, I'm thoroughly enjoying our tête-à-tête and I didn't mean to steer you off course."

 "Well, as for the rest of my 'growing up' years, prepare yourself for some campfire girl stories, summer lemonade stand fiascos and, later, four years of university study in a city that gave me a dose of culture shock. I must confess, though, city life was tempting after I graduated. I did consider sharing an apartment with one of my university friends, but, in the end, green pastures and wide, open spaces over-ruled. Guess I'm really a country girl at heart! Perhaps that chapter of my life can be told in another one of your rain-checks? Let's see, how many does that make so far"?

"I'm not counting, Laura, so take as many rain-checks as you like. About Paris, yes, I have to admit living and having been educated in Paris was an extraordinary experience. But the grass always looks greener on the other side of the fence. When you land on what you thought would be greener turf, you find as many weeds and imperfections as on the previous side. Life and people are the same wherever you go - only the scenery changes. That's just a small, personal observation. For me, the Alsace Lorraine region of France held more appeal than Paris, for it offers all of the sophisticated amenities of Paris, but in a more laid back, unpretentious sort of way.   Guess that makes me a seasoned country boy at heart. I can't wait to hear all about your campfire girl stories – not to mention your cat, Cuddles - and are you sure you don't have a pet chicken stashed away somewhere"?

"Well, I might – you'll just have to wait and see! Seriously – silliness aside, all I can say is welcome home, John Cavanaugh, it's nice to have you back. Our community needs someone like you – left handed compliments included"!

"Whoa there, Laura, let's get out on that ice – before I turn as red as the dress you're wearing! Besides, the orchestra is about to begin its medley of Viennese waltzes. So, Miss
Lady in Red, may I have the honor of the first waltz"?

"Indeed, Mr. Cavanaugh, I'd be delighted," I replied while making a playful curtsy. The dimmed crimson lights created a surreal atmosphere as the orchestra began to play "The Skater's Waltz". Johnny smiled as I slipped my arm into his and we began to skate.

Entranced in melodic reverie, we ignored the flashing camera that kept following us. Later that evening, Johnny announced that he would be starting his internship at Mother Cabrini hospital in the adjoining town.

The New Year promised many happy moments for Johnny and me. Winter week-ends were spent skating on the lake with our friends. During the summer months, the opulent estate served as a backdrop for the performing arts. Evenings we dined alfresco on the great lawn, lulled by a mixture of summer sounds and gentle breezes, under a canopy of stars. The seasons melded with sweet nostalgia.

One Year Later

As The Skater's Ball drew closer on the social horizon, Johnny wasn't his usual gregarious self. He was pensive, and, at times, agitated. He blamed his behavior on the long hours he had to spend at the hospital. Then, finally, after some prodding, he apologized and mentioned that he had been expecting a very important parcel that was to be shipped from abroad - - - something he wanted to use the night of the ball and had not yet received it. Since the ball was now only two days away, he was worried and questioned whether it would arrive on time.

St. Nicholas Eve

After all of the festivities had ended and St. Nicholas bid everyone a goodnight, Johnny invited our friends to his home for breakfast. After we had finished eating, everyone gathered around the tree in the parlor to sing carols when the doorbell rang. When I opened the door, Johnny was standing in the doorway with an impish grin on his face, holding a package tied with a large red bow.
"Hi Laura, Happy St. Nicholas Day, this is for you," he exclaimed, while handing me the package. Speechless, I followed him into the parlor where I hurriedly opened the gift. Under layers of red tissue lay two exquisitely crafted miniatures -The Victoria Palace and St. Mark's Cathedral.
 "Johnny, these are incredible", I gasped. "They're perfect replicas of my two favorite places. However did you do this"?

"I'm glad you asked! Now I can confess and reveal all of the mystery behind my questionable behavior - - particularly the anxiety I felt concerning this year's St. Nicholas Eve waiting for this package. It finally arrived in the nick of time, via DHL this morning.

But before I begin, I want everyone to get comfortable while I go into the kitchen and whip up some cappuccino to serve with the pastry that Laura's mother baked. I don't want anyone having hunger pangs in the middle of my story. Besides, that pastry has been waiting long enough to be enjoyed! Believe me when I tell you this pastry was well worth the wait. Laura's mother calls it her *crème de la crème* of desserts – so be prepared for a special treat.

Mariel remarked – "Are you kidding? No one could possibly have hunger pangs after that divinely French menu you prepared. The quiche and soufflé were beyond delicious.   Johnny, I must say Paris served you well, for you have become a chef extraordinaire!
All I want to do now is curl up on this divan with a cup of cappuccino and ready myself for a winter night's tale. I'm sure it's going to be quite a story. So begin - - *please!!* - - you have all of us suspended in suspense".

Rome –1998

"My story begins in Rome one afternoon in mid July. In a strange and curious way, fate intervened. Before leaving Europe, I wanted to visit The Eternal City once again, even though I had been there many times. In retrospect, I believe it was the hand of destiny that led me to the Fontana di Trevi, where this evening began to unfold.

Feeling like a foolish schoolboy, I closed my eyes and tossed a coin into the fountain, while making a wish. As I was leaving, I stopped to admire a miniature sculpture of St. Peter's Basilica.   It was an amazing piece of craftsmanship – the likes of which I had never seen before. As I was admiring it, the artist began to explain how he created the miniatures from photographs that he had taken. Thence began a friendly and lengthy chat. During our conversation, he made a sudden and unexpected prediction. Quite assuredly, he told me that my wish would come true. It startled me and I had a strange feeling that he knew exactly what I had wished for. Sensing my surprise, he quickly made a joke of it and assured me that he was not some weird warlock – only that he had a strong sense I would be blessed – as in the song, "Three Coins in the Fountain."

His dark eyes sparkled with merriment as we both broke into laughter. The mood immediately lightened. He then invited me to visit his studio that evening where I could see more of his artwork.

When I arrived at his home that evening, I was greeted with the warmest Italian hospitality. Antonio immediately un-corked a fine bottle of wine. Then, with flamboyant gusto, he escorted me to the adjoining room where an assortment of appetizers, various dishes of pasta and fish were displayed on a long table, draped in crisp white linen. A large, informal bouquet of various colored roses graced the center of the table. He laughed when he again saw my surprise at the elaborate setting.   Giving me a friendly pat on the back, Antonio quickly quoted some of his favorite Italian food proverbs”:

“Anche l’occhio vuole la sua parte:
The eyes want their part in the sense that something has to be pleasing to the eyes, apart from having other qualities.

Paese che vai, usanza che trovi:
Different places you visit - different customs you will find.
When in Italy, my friend, you dine also with your eyes. The presentation of food is just as important as the food itself. Now you can see how important dining is to an Italian. Now for the last proverb, which is my favorite - - and, I feel, is the most important one of all.

Uno non puo pensare bene, amare bene, dormire bene, se non ha mangiato bene:
One cannot think well, love well - sleep well, if one hasn’t eaten well.

There you have it, Giovanni, and I hope I have sufficiently explained the Italian custom of dining, because I have run out of proverbs! Besides – when I talk too much, I eat too much!   Come - - and as they say in America - - dig in!! - - our piccolo cena is waiting”!

“The evening proceeded with a mixture of delectable food, Roman history, opera and jazz music, interspersed with rollicking laughter and much wine into the late hours of the evening.

After our small dinner, as Antonio referred to our feast, he led me to a large, secluded room in the back of his home that served as his studio.

There he showed me his extensive collection. As I cast my eyes on his creations, I felt humbled and privileged to have met Antonio. He is one of the most fascinating characters I have ever met.

That evening offered me the most memorable moments I had ever experienced during my entire stay in Europe - particularly Rome - - and sealed the beginning of a new and lasting friendship.

Now for the final chapter of my story - - which takes place at last year's ball.

Laura, do you remember the photographer who kept following us last year, taking our picture"?
"Do I remember!!?? Silly question, how could I possibly forget! Every time we were skating, the photographer was either in front of us or behind us snapping our picture. It was like having our own paparazzo the entire evening – and it didn't seem to bother you at all"!

Johnny began to laugh.
"I had hired the photographer to take photos of The Victoria Palace and St. Mark's Cathedral – also the two of us skating. Then I sent the photographs to Antonio so he could make these miniatures for you. I wanted to give you something special for St. Nicholas Day, a gift that would be as meaningful to you, as your gift had been to me. I hope I've succeeded".

"Well my devious devil, you couldn't have chosen a more perfect gift. They're really beautiful, Johnny, they're so original - and so distinguished. You must tell Antonio how much I appreciate his artistry. I'll cherish them forever".

"Does that mean you'll forgive me for being such a devious devil?"
"Well, I don't know about *that* - - I'll have to give *that* some more thought! By the way, was Antonio right, did your wish come true"?

Mariel immediately chimed in.
"That was a fascinating story, Johnny, – but we all want to know if your wish came true - - so please - - don't keep us in suspense another minute - - tell us"!

Johnny smiled as he picked up The Victoria Palace and wound the little turn-key on the bottom. "Three Coins in the Fountain" began to tinkle melodiously as I peered through its tiny window. With amazement, I watched Johnny and I glide across the glittering ice, enshrouded forever in a crimson legacy.